ERLING HAALAND

BEN LERWILL

FOOTBALL LEGENDS

ERLING HAALAND

SCHOLASTIC

Published in the UK by Scholastic, 2024
1 London Bridge, London, SE1 9BG
Scholastic Ireland, 89E Lagan Road, Dublin Industrial Estate, Glasnevin, Dublin, D11 HP5F

SCHOLASTIC and associated logos are trademarks and/or registered trademarks of Scholastic Inc.

ISBN 978 0702 33325 5

A CIP catalogue record for this book is available from the British Library.

Printed and bound in Great Britain by Clays Ltd, Elcograf S.p.A

Paper made from wood grown in sustainable forests and other controlled sources.

3 5 7 9 10 8 6 4 2

While this book is based on real characters and actual historical events, some situations are fictional, created by the author.

UNAUTHORIZED: this book is not sponsored, approved or endorsed by any person who appears in this book.

www.scholastic.co.uk

Contents

MANCHESTER, 2002

In the players' lounge at Manchester City, a toddler was on the loose. The match had finished an hour ago, but this didn't matter to the two-year-old boy running around the room. He veered noisily from one side of the lounge to the other, bumping into grown-ups and bouncing off the walls.

The boy had a short mop of blond hair and a broad grin. He was wearing a child's replica kit, but even this was far too big for his small, chubby frame. The sleeves of the sky-blue shirt almost reached his wrists and his white shorts stretched down to his ankles.

The City team had changed and were here chatting with their families. The little boy looked around the room again, rubbed his nose, then carried on going wherever his legs carried him. As he hurried back through the crowd, the name and number on his shirt became visible. Above the number fifteen, it read "DAD".

The boy zigzagged through a maze of grown-ups then – bump! – he ran straight into the back of a strong pair of legs. The man they belonged to looked down. The boy, feeling a little dazed, looked up.

"Hello," said the man, chuckling. "What's the rush?"

The boy didn't know what to say, so just smiled.

"Hey, Alfie!" continued the man, calling to one of his teammates. "Your young boy's got plenty of energy!"

"Tell me something I don't know!" came the laughing response.

When the player looked down again, the toddler was already back on the move. The lounge was full of famous faces – footballers with trophies and medals, goal scorers whose names were known around the country – but for the boy scurrying among them, it was just a fun place to be.

None of them would have guessed, on that afternoon long ago, that the most successful footballer in the room wouldn't be anyone who had played that day.

Or that the name that would become best known around the world didn't belong to any of the adult players, but to the tiny boy causing mischief in the middle of them.

One day, this toddler would be back in Manchester.

His name was Erling, and he was something special.

A HOUSE OF SPORT

On Friday 21 July, 2000, one of the hottest days of the year, a boy named Erling Braut Haaland was born in the city of Leeds, England.

From the very beginning, sport was in his blood. His father, Alfie Haaland, was one of the most successful Norwegian footballers of his generation, a hard-tackling midfielder who played more than thirty times for his country. He spent most of his career in England, playing for Nottingham Forest, Leeds United and Manchester City.

You might think one superstar parent would be enough. But no. Erling's mother, Gry Marita Braut, was a professional athlete who had once been the champion of Norway in the heptathlon.

For female athletes, the heptathlon is the ultimate challenge. To be the best, you need strength, stamina, speed and skill. Gry Marita had all of these things – and the baby who arrived in the summer of 2000 would be blessed with them too.

"A healthy baby boy," said Gry Marita happily when they brought Erling home for the first time. "I could feel him kicking before he was born!"

The Haaland household in England was a lively one. There were always games to play, meals to prepare, and guests to welcome. Erling was the youngest of three children. His brother, Astor, was five years older and already a football nut. His sister, Gabrielle, was just two years older than baby Erling but always tottering around with her toys.

The youngest boy learned to get involved in whatever was going on – waddling across the garden after his siblings, or trailing his mum from room to room.

Alfie had just made an exciting move from Leeds United to Manchester City. His new manager, Joe Royle, thought so highly of him that he was made captain in his first season. As Alfie got into the routine of daily training, little Erling and the rest of the family busied themselves in other ways.

But the City training ground and the Haaland family home had one big thing in common. In both places, there were always footballs to be found. The children loved spending time in the garden, where they had a little net to shoot balls into. Astor was usually the loudest, dashing around the garden and imagining he was a Premier League star.

But he was a caring brother, and as Erling became more confident on his feet, Astor always involved him. "Here you go, little bro," he said one afternoon, rolling the ball to his brother. "Take some shots at me."

Alfie and Gry Marita were in the kitchen, preparing a lasagna for tea. "The meal's ready," said Alfie. "I'll go and call the boys." But Gry Marita touched his arm. "Wait," she said, gazing out of the window. "Look."

As they watched from the kitchen, little Erling took a run-up at the ball he'd placed on the ground. He took one step, two steps, then – pow! – he swung his left foot and sent the ball whooshing past Astor's right hand. Alfie and Gry Marita looked at each other, their eyes widening.

Happy with his first shot, Erling scampered to collect the ball and placed it back on the grass. He was grinning like a boy who had just been given a surprise present. He ran up again. This time the ball sailed even harder and faster into the net. Now Astor was grinning too. "Wow!" he said.

After Erling had booted the ball into the goal for the third time, the boys looked around to see their dad smiling broadly. "OK, you two, it's teatime," Alfie said. Then he bent down to ruffle Erling's bright blond hair. The tiny boy was barely up to his dad's knees. "We're going to have to keep you well fed, goal machine."

BACK TO NORWAY

Alfie's career with City lasted three seasons. The family felt at home in England, and the City fans loved having Alfie in their squad, but injuries had stopped him from playing regular football. And after being on the end of a painful tackle from Roy Keane in the Manchester derby, his career was as good as over.

This put the family in a difficult position. They were settled in England, but their true home lay in Norway. "We have to make a decision," said Gry Marita. They started talking about Bryne, the small farming town where they had both grown up. They remembered their own happy childhoods. They also knew that by going back there, they would be closer to friends and family. Before long, they'd made their minds up. "It's best for the kids, and best for us," said Alfie.

The Haaland children all had brilliant memories of their time in England – of outings to the countryside, and matchday trips to Manchester City's famous old Maine Road stadium – but they were excited about their big move to Norway. "It's going to be an adventure!" said Gabrielle.

Bryne even had its own professional football team, called Bryne FK, who Alfie had played for much earlier in his career. They were in Norway's First Division, and the players wore bright red shirts, just like the national team. There was no doubt which club the Haaland family would be supporting when they moved back.

When the day of the move arrived, their house was a whirl of activity. People trooped in and out, filling a huge lorry outside with packing boxes. The rooms that Erling was familiar with now looked different – the sitting room had no sofas or TV, and the kitchen had no chairs or table.

He clutched his backpack, in which he'd packed all his special books and toys. Poking out of the top was a blue soft toy with pointy ears and alien eyes. This was Moonchester, the Manchester City mascot. Erling wasn't leaving his favourite cuddly toy behind.

Just a few days later, Erling watched the boxes being loaded into their new house in Bryne. He felt happy, but also a bit unsure about being somewhere new. Alfie saw that his youngest son was deep in thought. "This is our home now," he said, as they spotted a group of uncles, aunts and cousins walking towards the house. "Welcome to Bryne, Erling."

As the three Haaland children settled into their new life in Bryne, sport continued to feature heavily. Gry Marita and Alfie always encouraged them to do the best they could, no matter which sport they were playing. "There's no better feeling than being proud of yourself," said Gry Marita. "And the most important thing – have fun, too!"

Erling listened closely to this advice. He was enjoying himself at school and getting the chance to try lots of different sports. By the time he was five, he was already good at cross-country skiing and handball. And much to his mum's delight, he was also an excellent little athlete.

At school, when the children played chase games in the playground, none of his young friends could keep up with him. The PE teacher had noticed the smiley blond boy speeding around the school, but there was one morning when Erling really caught his eye.

"I want you all to try doing a standing long jump into this sandpit," said the teacher. As the children lined up, he demonstrated. "Stand on this line, bend your knees, swing your arms back, then jump forward as far as you can. Good luck!"

Little Erling watched the rest of his class have a go then stepped up. He followed the instructions, bending his legs then springing into the sandpit. The teacher raised his eyebrows and made a note on his pad. Erling thought he might have done well, but he was still surprised when the teacher took him to one side. "Erling," he said. "I'd like you to join the local athletics club."

This was exciting news – there was an athletics competition the very next weekend. On the morning of the competition, Erling was up early with his sports kit on. Gry Marita showed him some stretching exercises, and soon it was time to go. He laced up his trainers and bounded out to the car.

When they got to the athletics track, Erling headed straight to the long-jump pit. Other boys and girls were already waiting there, getting ready to jump. The judge – a man in a white cap – was raking the pit. One by one, the children came forward, bent their knees, and leaped as far as they could into the sand.

Again, Erling waited for his turn until his name was called. An orange marker in the pit showed the longest jump so far. He looked at his mum and waved. Then he crouched down, swung his arms and launched himself forward, stretching his heels out.

He landed in the sand – sploosh! When he picked himself up, he realized he'd gone way beyond the orange marker. So far beyond it, in fact, that the judge looked shocked. The man adjusted his cap and checked his tape measure. "That's … wow! That's one metre, sixty-three centimetres. I think that's the longest jump I've ever seen."

Little Erling went home delighted. He'd won! Gry Marita told him how proud she was. But there was a further surprise in store. The judge visited the Haaland family the next morning. "I've checked the figures. Erling's jump wasn't just the longest in Bryne," said the man, beaming. "It was the longest standing jump by a five-year-old anywhere, ever. It's a world record!"

Standing next to his parents, who could barely believe what they were hearing, Erling started hopping up and down excitedly. Winning had felt great, but this felt even better. His dad kneeled beside him and laughed happily.

"Incredible! Just incredible!" Alfie said. Then he smiled. "You know, son, I have a feeling this won't be the last time you do something special."

FOOTBALL TAKES OVER

Despite having a talent for so many different sports, young Erling had one obsession.

Morning, afternoon and evening, he could be found with a football – dribbling around the chairs in the kitchen, trying keepie-uppies in the garden, playing headers in the park. Wherever he was, a ball was never far away. He collected football stickers, too, swapping them with his friends at school, always desperate to add the big-name strikers to his collection.

At home, Alfie often had the television on, watching live games from other European countries.

This only added to Erling's fascination. He liked nothing better than joining his dad on the sofa to watch forwards like Didier Drogba, Zlatan Ibrahimovic and Samuel Eto'o. They never gave up and could turn a game with a moment of brilliance. The football they played was fast and dramatic. Erling loved watching them.

His enjoyment of the game didn't go unnoticed in Bryne. It was a small town, where many people knew the Haaland family. Word started spreading that Erling might make a good youth team player.

"I have something to tell you," said Alfie one morning over breakfast. Erling, who was looking at a football magazine while eating big spoonfuls of porridge, looked up quizzically. "You're going to be joining a children's training session at the Bryne FK academy next week. Just a little try-out. What do you think about that?"

Erling's jaw dropped. The porridge on his spoon plopped back into the bowl. "At the academy?" he said. "Dad, that's the best news ever!"

He couldn't wait. Joining a proper training session at an academy was unbelievably exciting – this was his dad's former club, after all; a real football club! – and when the day arrived, he sprang out of the car clutching his boots.

Erling and his dad walked towards what looked like a big sports hall. As Alfie began chatting to the people inside, Erling's eyes were drawn to a row of framed team photos.

He heard a kind voice at his side. "So you're Alfie's young boy," said a smiling man in glasses and a tracksuit. "I'm the youth coach here at Bryne. My name's Alf Ingve Berntsen. Welcome to the academy."

Ten minutes later Erling was inside the hall, surrounded by other young boys and girls. Scattered around them were balls, nets and cones. Erling smiled at two or three of the other players who he recognized from school, but when he was handed an orange bib and told that a practice match was about to start, he still felt a bit nervous.

"Hello, I'm Tord," said one of his teammates, a boy with brown hair and a big grin. "And I'm Andrea," added another, a friendly girl with a ponytail. "If I get the ball, I'll try to pass it to you," she said.

Sure enough, the first time Andrea had possession she looked up to see where Erling was.

Her pass came straight to his feet. He saw that Tord was running into space, so he waited for the right moment then side-footed the ball into his teammate's path. Tord tried a shot. The keeper caught it with both hands.

"Unlucky, Tord!" shouted Coach Berntsen. "Great passing, Andrea and Erling!"

The team soon had another chance. Tord won the ball and looked around. This time it was Erling's turn to make a run. As his teammate sent the ball forward, it bounced right in front of him. Suddenly, he had just the keeper to beat. He swung his left foot through the ball and watched as it looped into the net.

"Gooooaaaalll! What a finish!" shouted Andrea, rushing up to congratulate him. "Wonderful stuff!" said Coach Berntsen. Erling felt a buzz of joy. As he ran back into position, eager for the chance to score more, he looked up to his dad on the sidelines. Alfie gave his son a big thumbs-up.

Playing at the academy was going to be fun, thought Erling. Really fun.

MOVING ON UP

The academy hall at Bryne soon felt like a second home for Erling. By the time he was eight, he moved up from doing one training session a week to two. The indoor pitch was a great place to practice during the cold, icy Norwegian winters, and the outdoor pitches were perfect for training and five-a-sides during summer. Coach Berntsen had three simple rules: be on time, do your best and behave. Rain, snow or sun, Erling would be there with a ball at his feet and a smile on his face.

He enjoyed every aspect of the training sessions: the warm-up exercises, the shooting drills, the fitness tests and the dribbling practice. But best of all he loved the matches, particularly against other academy teams. This was when he could really shine.

"That was immense, Erling!" said Tord after a game against the local champions, when Erling had scored the winner. "You're the top scorer in the league!"

Erling really liked the other young players – they were keen and determined, just like him – and he trusted them as teammates as well as friends. When he pulled on his red Bryne shirt and lined up next to them, he felt part of something special. And although he was still small, his simple, fist-pump goal celebration was already a familiar sight on youth pitches around the region.

"That's Erling Haaland," the spectators would say to each other. "Alfie's youngest son. Have you seen how skilful he is? He's one to watch, and no mistake."

When he first started at the academy, he hadn't given much thought to his best position. He just loved playing football. The coaches often played him on the left wing, because his left foot was his strongest weapon, but as time went by it became obvious to everyone: a goal machine like Erling just had to be a striker.

At a match shortly after his tenth birthday, when he scored four and set up another three, Coach Berntsen spoke to him. "That was amazing today, Erling," he said. "The third goal – wow! And with your right foot! You showed some really great link-up play too."

Erling was out of breath from the game. "I've been thinking," continued the coach. "When you're playing, we often win 7-0 or 8-0. I'd like you to think about joining the year group above, so you can really challenge yourself."

Erling loved being on a team with his friends, but the idea of being good enough to play against older children made his chest swell with happiness. He was starting to dream of being a professional – even, in his wildest moments, a Champions League player – and this seemed like a great step forward.

"It's your decision," said Gry Marita and Alfie that evening, as the family had dinner. Erling had come straight home and started firing balls into the goal in the garden. Sitting at the table was the first time the boy had paused all day. "We'll support you in whatever you want to do, so it's up to you."

For young Erling, who was busy devouring his meal and imagining the future, his mind was already made up.

BRYNE FK

Club name: Bryne FK
Nickname: Jaerens Superlag (the Super Team from the Jaerens Region)
Founded: April 1926
Current league: Norwegian First Division
Current manager: Kevin Knappen
Crest: A red globe in a white shield on the outline of a green leaf, with the words 'Bryne FK'

HOMETOWN MURALS

Erling might be a global superstar, but he hasn't been forgotten in Bryne, where some of his talented fans have made murals (large outdoor paintings) to honour him. On a building near the train station, a giant mural has been painted showing Erling celebrating in his Dortmund kit. Elsewhere in Bryne, a smaller mural shows him taking a pig for a walk on a lead! It reminds people that Erling comes from a humble farming town.

A RISING STAR

When Erling was thirteen, a Norwegian TV crew arrived at a Bryne academy game. They'd heard about the young star with a blond buzzcut, a big smile and a shot like a rocket. Erling wasn't affected by the TV cameras and played brilliantly, twice whipping the ball into the back of the net. The crew interviewed him after the match.

"Erling, you scored two goals," said the interviewer. "Where did you learn this? From your dad?"

Erling, whose cheeks were still red from the match, grinned from ear to ear as his teammates clustered around to listen. "I don't know." He chuckled. "I learned by myself."

This was true – but only partly. Erling was still fanatical about watching football on the TV and often asked his dad about the forwards he'd played with in England. He loved hearing Alfie's stories about City players like Shaun Goater, who scored more than a hundred times by being brave and persistent, and Nicholas Anelka, another striker who was famed for his lightning-quick pace.

It got Erling thinking about what qualities made the perfect striker. At weekends he and his friends often rode their bikes the five minutes down to the academy pitches to kick balls around, even when there were no coaches about. Erling imagined he was strong, muscular forwards like Zlatan Ibrahimović or Cristiano Ronaldo. He was growing, but his shirt still hung loose from his shoulders and his legs were skinny. He didn't yet have the brute strength to go with his skills.

But what skills they were! Every week he worked hard on his shooting, his heading and his ability to find space. This last one was the trickiest of the lot, but he was starting to master how to be in the right place at the right time. At training sessions, where he was often barged about by older, stronger defenders, he was constantly learning more about tactics and technique.

"Yes, Erling!" shouted Coach Berntsen after one neatly slotted goal. "Great positioning. You waited for just the right moment to drift away from your marker!"

By now, his reputation was spreading way beyond Bryne. Some of his teammates were even saying he should be selected for Norway's Under-15 squad. "They'd be mad not to pick you," said his friend Steffen. "You're one of the best players in our league!"

Sure enough, a letter from the Norwegian FA soon dropped through the Haalands' letterbox. Erling was in his bedroom playing FIFA with his friends when a voice came up the stairs.

"Erling," shouted Gabrielle. "There's some post for you!"

He rushed downstairs to open it. Erling's talents had been noticed by the national selectors – he was being invited to join the Under-15 squad! This was like nothing he'd ever felt before. His dreams of becoming a professional footballer were getting closer – and he would be wearing the red national shirt!

Soon he found himself as a regular member of the Norway youth set-up. The players around him were quicker and more skilful than his academy teammates, and the opposing teams were more organized and physical. "Just play your own game," advised his dad. "Believe in yourself. Give it everything and you'll see the results."

When Erling lined up for his country against Sweden's Under-15 team, he tried to put this advice into action. But it wasn't easy. The first half was tough work. He kept pressing the centre-backs, but by half-time he was frustrated by his lack of chances.

As they came back for the second half, Erling approached one of his teammates, a defender called Colin. By coincidence, Colin's dad had also been a Manchester City player – the striker Uwe Rosler – so the two boys had connected from the moment they'd met. "I've noticed their keeper coming off his line," whispered Erling. "I think I might try something. Watch."

Colin went to his position, wondering what Erling meant. He soon found out. When the ball was tapped back from the kick-off, Erling took one step forward and hammered a shot goalwards from the halfway line. The ball sailed over the entire Swedish team and dipped under the crossbar, leaving the goalkeeper in a panicked heap.

GOOOAAALLLL!!!!!

The Norway players and substitutes went bananas, mobbing Erling. Even Erling himself couldn't quite believe his plan had worked. Straight after the match, his dad came up to give him a big hug. "Now that's what I call believing in yourself!" He laughed.

Erling grinned and looked around. There had only been a few people in the stands to witness his goal, but he felt ecstatic. This small ground was a far cry from the packed stadiums of the big European leagues, but one thing was for sure – he was moving in the right direction.

Before the match he had fantasized to Colin about one day playing for the Manchester City first team. Even now, he still bought all the latest City replica shirts. The boys had giggled about it together as they put on their shin-pads.

But maybe, thought Erling, playing on the biggest

stage wasn't such a fantasy after all. He just had to keep working.

CLIMBING THE LADDER

As Erling became taller and more confident, things moved fast. First he was promoted into the Bryne reserve team, where as a lanky fifteen-year-old he looked out of place among the broad-shouldered adults. Most of his new teammates were friendly, but some seemed grumpy that someone so young was playing alongside them. On top of this, Erling found that the whole pace of the game was faster, and more of a battle.

But as he got used to the tempo of the matches, Erling realized that he, too, was a battler, and that if he got stuck in and played his natural game, scoring still came easily. In the fourteen matches he played for the reserves, he scored eighteen times!

For Erling, goals had become addictive. Whenever he put the ball in the net – whether it was through a scrappy header, a one-on-one or a long-range screamer – all he wanted to do was score again.

"It's like I'm always hungry," he explained to Astor after a match one summer evening, as they lay on their backs in the garden. "But when I score, it doesn't go away. It makes me hungrier!"

Despite Erling's age, his ability meant it was only a matter of time before he got a first team call-up. It came two months before his sixteenth birthday, in a match against Ranheim. The match was one of sixteen first-team games he played for Bryne, but for the first time in his life, the goals dried up.

For some players, this would have destroyed their self-belief. Not Erling. He felt down about it, but rather than seeing it as a disaster, he saw it as an opportunity. After all, here he was, a fifteen-year old playing in Norway's First Division. He took the chance to improve other parts of his game: running hard, tracking back, helping the team to work as a unit. He was also getting used to playing in front of crowds.

"Good work, young lad! Keep going!" the fans shouted whenever he slid in with a tackle or sprinted to block a pass. There was more to being a striker, Erling was realizing, than goals and assists.

And his constant desire to win, coupled with his natural talent, soon attracted the attention of scouts from Molde FK, one of the best teams in the country.

Erling heard the news one winter's day, after a match for the Bryne first team. He'd raced tirelessly around the cold pitch all afternoon, closing down defenders and refusing to be muscled off the ball. When Coach Berntsen approached him after the game, Erling thought he would be hearing the usual encouragement. But the coach had something else to say – and Erling's mouth fell open when he heard what it was.

"A bid from Molde! For me!" Erling gasped. "But they were Norwegian champions just two seasons ago!"

There was great excitement when he told his parents the news. This was an incredible opportunity – but also a nerve-racking one. Molde was around 400 kilometres north of Bryne, and Erling would be moving up there alone, aged just sixteen. His parents had taught him how to look after himself, but the prospect was still daunting.

"We'll support you in whatever you choose," said Gry Marita that evening. They were all elated at the thought of Erling playing for a top-flight club. "Just promise me you'll remember to wash your socks!"

There was another reason why a move to Molde was so appealing to Erling. The club manager was Ole Gunnar Solskjaer, who had played up front for Manchester United and Norway. Erling would be learning from one of the best.

"But are you sure you want to be managed by an ex-United player?" joked Astor, clapping his younger brother on the shoulder. Erling laughed and thought of the City kits in his bedroom drawer. "Well, at least Molde wear blue!" he replied.

A few weeks later, after talking things over with his family, he embarked on the biggest step in his career to date. Moving to Molde with just a few sports bags filled with his favourite clothes, he was now officially a top-flight footballer.

That night, as he lay down in his new bedroom, he breathed deep. This was a major moment in his life.

The future seemed clearer now, his dreams more real. He just had to stay focused. He set his alarm for the next morning – he would, as normal, be waking up to the sound of the Champions League anthem – and closed his eyes. *Keep calm,* Erling told himself. *You've got this.*

MOLDE FK

Nickname: MFK
Founded: June 1911
Current league: Eliteserien (Norwegian Premier League)
Current manager: Erling Moe
Crest: A blue oval with white trim, with the letters MFK and the numbers 19/6/1911 (the date the club was founded)

"I'm Ole," said the manager the next morning, striding across the training ground with a big smile. He held out his hand for Erling to shake. "Welcome to Molde."

Erling tried hard not to get over-excited. Ole had once scored the winner in a Champions League final. Now he was Erling's boss! Everything here looked professional – the lines were freshly painted, the nets were new, even the bibs were dazzlingly bright. It all felt right.

His new teammates were high-quality, too. Erling was shy when he first met them, but as the weeks went by, he began to play with more freedom. They loved his enthusiasm.

"I'm learning loads from the players here," said Erling on the phone to his dad one night. "They're strong tacklers! I'm really trying to make the most of each session. I scored a great header today in training. It feels good here, Dad."

"You've got the right attitude," said Alfie. "Keep training hard, keep playing hard. And remember what your mum always says: keep enjoying yourself!"

Erling soon felt settled and happy in Molde, but he missed his life in Bryne. A few months earlier, he and two friends had formed a rap band called the Flow Kingz. They'd even made a video, messing about in the sunshine, laughing and doing the things that teenage boys do. Now he was away from both his family and his mates. He was sixteen, but suddenly felt like a grown-up.

He acted like one on the pitch, too. Two months after his move, he made his first-team debut in an away cup match against Volda TI. The match was a messy one, with a goalless first half, but his chance to get on the scoresheet came at the start of the second.

Breaking down the left, Erling ran on to a through-ball. Immediately, he knew a chance was on. His first touch steered him away from the defenders and into the area. There was just the keeper to beat – all it needed was a finish. He drew back his left foot and shot. GOAL!

He raised his arm in celebration. The relief he felt was huge. After a busy second half, Molde won the game 3-2, with Erling playing a big part in the victory. His older teammates were full of praise at the end, as was Ole. Erling's career at Molde was up and running.

His drive and attitude meant he got plenty more game time as the season progressed, making twenty appearances. He was growing mentally – but his physical growth was even more impressive. He was at the age where his body seemed to be expanding by the week. His chest was becoming fuller, his legs chunkier, and his arms stronger.

By the time he lined up in the cup quarter-final against Kristiansund a few months after his debut, he had a new nickname from his teammates: Man-Child. The name made Erling happy. The skinny boy of last season was gone – defenders had to deal with his height and strength now.

Thousands of fans were in the stadium. Molde went a goal down early on and looked beaten, but there was a twist to come. In the seventy-fourth minute, they broke down the right. Erling positioned himself in the box, waiting for a cross. When it came, he was ready. He burst free of his marker, leaped into the air and sent the perfect header into the far corner.

The fans went wild. So did Erling, roaring at the crowd. Three minutes later, Molde scored again to take a 2-1 lead. When the final whistle went, the players were overjoyed. Erling sprinted over and got swept into the blue-shirted huddle. "Yes, Man-Child!" shouted Ante, their goalkeeper. "We did it!"

Erling finished the season with four goals and a

whole army of new fans, but even he was surprised by what was next in store. At one training session he'd noticed some of the Molde coaches talking among themselves and looking in his direction, but it was Ole himself who broke the news.

"Erling," he said, with a wry smile. "There's something you need to know. It's not great for my future plans, but it's also not surprising."

Ole explained that Erling had been spotted by RB Salzburg, the biggest team in Austria. It was soon arranged that he would be spending one more season at Molde, then making a big transfer overseas. He would be playing in a 30,000-seat stadium in Salzburg, for a team which was regularly in the Champions League. The thought made him dizzy.

The boy from Bryne was going places.

RB SALZBURG

Nickname: Die Roten Bullen (The Red Bulls)
Founded: September 1933
Current league: Austrian Bundesliga
Current manager: Gerhard Struber
Crest: A white shield with black trim under a yellow star, with two bulls charging towards a football

ON CLOUD NINE

"I can't believe how big you've grown!" said Gry Marita, hugging her son as he stepped into the family home. Erling now towered over his mum. He was well over six feet tall and growing bigger and more powerful all the time. "I ate some magic beans in Molde," he joked, as he embraced her.

Erling looked around. "It feels really good to be back home for a while," he said. Then he sniffed the air. "Wait," he smiled, "do I smell Dad's lasagna?"

Alfie appeared from the kitchen, a tea towel over one shoulder. "Of course!" he laughed. "When my boy's back home, he gets his favourite meal!"

Erling didn't often get the chance to come back home, but when he did, he jumped at it. He was now midway through his second season with Molde and had been banging in goals for months. Just a few weeks ago he'd scored four times in the first twenty-one minutes of an away match against Brann, including a coolly taken penalty in front of the home fans. And he was still only seventeen!

Now, back in Bryne, he was being recognized in the street. Kids kept coming up to him to ask for autographs and selfies. "You're doing us proud," said the woman behind the counter at his favourite bakery, handing him a bag of oatmeal cookies. "Good luck next year in Austria!"

He spent the next day hanging out with his old friends, playing FIFA and howling with laughter as they remembered their schooldays. Erling listened closely when they talked about their plans for the future. They wanted to become boat-builders, doctors and teachers.

Erling's life was mapped out very differently. His upcoming transfer to RB Salzburg was now well known. His friends were delighted for him, he could tell, and that made him happy. But only Erling knew exactly how much it meant to him.

He finished his second season at Molde as top scorer, helping the club finish second in the league. But when he officially joined RB Salzburg on 1 January 2019, it signalled the start of an even more amazing year. He knew he was stepping into a new world, with more pressure, more fans and more publicity. But he didn't let this bother him. In fact, he thrived on it.

This was just as well – because life was about to get turbo-charged.

Erling arrived in Salzburg in the heart of the Austrian winter. As soon as his plane landed among the snowy mountains, he knew he'd made a good move. The air felt clean and the city felt friendly. The fans were loud and loyal. RB Salzburg themselves, meanwhile, were top of the league and had players from all over the world. Erling knew he would fit right in.

He had watched the team playing on TV whenever he could, so he already recognized many of the faces on the training pitch. He even felt a little starstruck. Over there was Takumi Minamino, the Japanese forward. He was practicing quick passes with Dominik Szoboszlai, the Hungarian midfielder. Stretching next to them was André Ramalho, the Brazilian centre-back. Erling took a deep breath, zipped up his red Salzburg training top, and jogged across.

"I'm really excited you're here," said Takumi, walking over to greet him. He was a full eight inches shorter than Erling, but he was calm and assured. "Me too," said Erling, who knew how skilful Takumi was.

During practice, the pair of them combined well, picking each other out with flicks and through-balls. Erling knew he'd found someone he would enjoy playing with.

But his first few months in Austria were about finding his feet. He worked on his language skills, kept himself fit and got to know his teammates. The season was already close to finishing when he joined, and although he made five appearances – scoring once, with his trusty left foot – his sights were set on the start of the next season. If all went well, he'd even be playing Champions League games!

In the meantime, he had another big challenge to focus on. The FIFA Under-20 World Cup was taking place in Poland, and Erling was a key member of the Norway squad. They'd been drawn in a group with Uruguay, New Zealand and Honduras.

As they travelled on the team bus to their opening game against Uruguay, Erling put his headphones on and tried to relax. He had played against most of his Norwegian squad mates while he was at Bryne and Molde. He knew they were good. He felt sure they could get beyond the group stages.

But the opposition had different plans. Uruguay beat them 3-1. Three days later, any dreams Norway had of doing well were shattered when they lost 2-0 to New Zealand. Erling was gutted. Played two, lost two. They were out of the tournament. Just one match remained, against Honduras, for them to rescue some pride.

"We've been terrible so far," said Erling before kick-off, gathering his teammates around him. He had an intense look in his eyes. "We need a big win to show people back home we're no losers. Let's do it!"

He led from the front, playing like a man on a mission. After just seven minutes, he side-footed a low cross into the net to give Norway the lead. By half-time they were 5-0 up and Erling had scored four, all with his left foot. The fans scattered around the stadium couldn't quite believe what they were watching – but Erling and his teammates weren't done yet.

As Norway ran and pressed, the goals kept coming. By the fiftieth minute they were winning 7-0 and Erling had scored another. He now had five. Surely he couldn't get a double hat-trick? Fifteen minutes later, his strike partner Kristian Thorstvedt dribbled the ball into the six-yard box and played it to Erling. He tapped it home, this time with his right. Six goals!

Astonishingly, more were to come. Over the next twenty minutes, Norway added three further goals, two of them from Erling. This was unbelievable. Even back in the Bryne academy, he'd never scored this many. He'd now bagged eight – eight! – and there were still a few minutes left.

As the final seconds played out, he found himself with one last chance. A pass was lifted through from midfield, finding Erling in space. He took two quick touches then unleashed a left-footed drive. It flew into the top corner. Norway had won 12-0 and Erling had scored NINE GOALS! A hat-trick of hat-tricks!

"That was insane! I nearly ran out of fingers to keep count!" joked Kristian as they headed back down the tunnel. Erling laughed. Their team might not have progressed, but he and Norway had shown the world what they could do. Two weeks later, he learned that he had won the tournament's Golden Boot trophy.

Back in Salzburg, he rested the award on a shelf above his bed. It looked amazing. And – he thought, as he tucked into a celebratory pizza and set his Champions League alarm for the next morning – it felt pretty amazing, too.

CHAMPIONS LEAGUE AT LAST

Erling settled into a cross-legged position on his bedroom floor, closed his eyes and let his shoulders loosen. As random distractions flickered across his mind, he let them pass, instead focusing on his breath.

In. Out. In. Out.

Soon he was in a state of calm, where thoughts floated away and nothing mattered except the rhythm of his breathing.

In. Out. In. Out.

It was one of his friends in Molde who had first encouraged him to try meditation. Erling had made it part of his daily life ever since. It helped him to stay in the moment, kept him relaxed and made it easier to deal with stress. His physical health was incredible; anyone could see that. He was all muscle. But Erling also knew how important it was to look after his mental health. That was where meditation came in.

As the new season got underway, he needed a clear head more than ever. Erling was now being admired by managers across Europe, from the German Bundesliga to the English Premier League. And he'd grown to six feet five inches tall: a giant teenager with a giant reputation.

He smashed in three goals for RB Salzburg in pre-season friendlies. Now, whenever he arrived at the stadium or the training ground, he was mobbed by young fans. He got used to having phones and TV cameras pointed at him wherever he turned. At matches, he heard his name being sung by thousands of fans at a time. It thrilled him, but staying composed was everything. He still checked the European football scores – and always kept an eye out for City's latest results in the Premier League – but his job was to focus on helping Salzburg.

And being calm didn't always mean being laid-back. He became an animal when the whistle blew. The defenders in the Austrian league didn't know what had hit them. Erling was impossible to mark. He hung back, darted forward, ran left, ran right, then exploded in a flurry of strength, speed and sharp shooting. The defenders would go one way and Erling would instinctively go the other. He was unstoppable, and the Salzburg fans loved it.

The goals poured in. Three against Parndorf, three against Wolfsberger, two against SKN St Polten. Eight matches into the season, he'd already scored fourteen times, frequently linking up with Takumi and new Korean signing, Hee-chan Hwang. Salzburg were clocking up victory after victory, much to the delight of their new manager Jesse Marsch.

But the ninth match of the season was the big one: a home Champions League game against Belgian champions Genk. This was the moment Erling had been dreaming of: his debut in the competition. His whole body tingled as he heard the familiar theme echoing around the ground before kick-off, the same music he'd woken up to each morning for years. The stadium was a frenzy of scarves, flags and red shirts.

His parents had flown out to watch him. He waved up to the stands, and as the teams lined up, his mum's words resounded in his ears. *Enjoy yourself.*

Just two minutes into the game, things erupted. Hee-chan received the ball on the edge of the box, jinked around a defender and laid it into Erling's path. In his mind, time seemed to freeze. This was the Champions League – the lights, the crowd, the cameras. This was now. With a defender at his back, he turned his body and swept the ball right-footed under the keeper. He'd scored!!

He sprinted along the touchline, yelling with joy, his arms outstretched. In the thirty-fourth minute he made it two, firing home from just inside the area, and as half-time approached he found the net again with a close-range tap-in. A first-half hat-trick on his Champions League debut. Was this really happening? The roar of the crowd, who watched Salzburg win 6-2, thundered in his ears. This was no dream.

When he turned his phone back on in the changing room, the words of congratulations came flooding in. There were dozens of messages from schoolfriends and former teammates, all singing his praises. His social-media channels were on fire with likes and emojis. His family, too, were jubilant.

"Incredible! We're all so proud of you," said Alfie, wrapping Erling in a bear hug that evening. "Just don't get carried away. Keep doing what you're doing."

The following few months were a blur of bulging nets and broken records. His next Champions League match was against the mighty Liverpool, at Anfield, where he finished off a brilliant team move in front of more than 50,000 fans. Against Napoli at home, he scored two more. He kept finding the net, soon becoming the first teenager to score in five consecutive Champions League games.

He hadn't slowed down in the league, either. When he hit another three goals against Wolfsberger in early November, it was his fifth hat-trick of the season. By early December, he'd played twenty-two games and scored twenty-eight goals. He even had seven assists to his name.

2019 had been an utterly extraordinary year for Erling – and the whole world of football was now sitting up and paying attention. He'd soon be on the move again.

THE YELLOW WALL

In Bryne, the Christmas Eve feast was well underway. Twelve members of the Haaland family were gathered noisily around the dining table, piling their plates with traditional Norwegian food.

Astor was dishing out hot, crispy potatoes to his cousins. Gry Marita was pouring glasses of wine. "Pass the pork ribs," shouted Alfie, "I can't get enough of them." Then he pointed across the table to his youngest son, who was watching the scene happily. "He's going to need some too if he wants to get the better of those Bundesliga defenders!"

Before the meal, Erling had broken the news

to his uncles, aunts and cousins. Less than a year after joining Salzburg, he had signed with Borussia Dortmund, one of the biggest clubs in Germany, for a twenty-million-euro fee. The next chapter was about to begin. His relatives had showered him with hugs and kisses. Erling was now a household name in Norway, where he was also playing and scoring regularly for the national team.

He picked up his fork and looked around. Life was good sometimes. Here in the family home, he felt like a regular guy from Bryne. But soon, he knew, the tough stuff would begin again.

Tough stuff? Who was he kidding? He couldn't wait to get started. The world-famous Bundesliga was waiting.

Ten days later he was on a chilly training pitch in Dortmund, shaking the hand of his new manager, Lucien Favre, and being introduced to some of Europe's top club professionals. He'd grown up watching big German players like Marco Reus, Mario Götze and Mats Hummels. Now they were his teammates, in the same yellow training kit. He was wowed by the facilities, too. Everything, from the players' restaurant to the changing rooms, was a step up from his previous clubs.

On his first practice drill, he was paired with the young English winger Jadon Sancho. "So what's it like here?" Erling asked, as they pinged the ball back and forth in the January drizzle. "It's the best," enthused Jadon. "The fans are incredible. The staff are excellent. This is a proper, proper football club."

Erling would have to wait a couple of weeks before experiencing his first home game, but he got a sense of things whenever he set foot outside. Journalists thronged around him in the training ground car park. Wherever he went, there were camera phones, crowds and excited cheers. Among the Dortmund fans, expectation was high. "You're one of the Black and Yellows now, Erling!" one man shouted from a car window. "Show us what you can do!"

Life moves fast when you're on the way up. Erling was learning this quicker than anyone. After one of his first training sessions, he'd seen his face staring back from a giant poster in the club shop window. The same afternoon, he'd seen himself smiling out from the front cover of Kicker, Germany's top sports magazine. He was big news. Erling closed his eyes, shook his head slightly, and smiled. It was unreal. *Stay focused*, he told himself. *Just keep doing your thing.*

His chance to do just that came a few days later, at an away match in front of 30,000 fans at Augsburg. He was named on the bench, and when he was brought on after fifty-five minutes, Dortmund were 3-1 down. All eyes turned to the tall blond substitute. Four minutes later, he drilled in a low shot from the edge of the area. Within twenty-five minutes, he had a hat-trick and Dortmund were closing in on a win.

"You make this look easy!" screamed Jadon as they celebrated Erling's third goal in front of the ecstatic away fans.

A week later, Erling witnessed the matchday atmosphere of the 80,000-capacity Westfalenstadion for the first time. The south stand was legendary as being the largest terraced grandstand in Europe, with enough space to hold 25,000 fans. Its nickname was the Yellow Wall – and you heard it before you saw it.

As Erling and the other players ran out, the Yellow Wall came to life, making a sound louder than anything he'd heard in a stadium. It was like rolling thunder. Scarves were being held up, chants were being sung, drums were being played. Even way up at the very top of the stand, it was packed with yellow-shirted fans. The whole stadium was a cauldron of noise. Erling looked around and mouthed "Wow".

Dortmund were playing Köln, who they beat easily. Erling was a substitute again, but he grabbed two goals when he came on, right in front of the Yellow Wall. The roar when he scored was ear-splitting. Dortmund won 5-1, moving to third in the table. This was the big time, and Erling had arrived.

The goals kept coming. Less than a month later, he'd scored nine times in six games, sending Europe's newspapers and football websites into overdrive. Foreign magazines came to interview him, as he tried his best to stay cheerful and cool-headed. But even Erling was dazzled by the match that was up next: a Champions League knock-out game against Paris Saint-Germain.

As the Dortmund team bus arrived at Westfalenstadion on the night of the game, he scrolled through the good luck messages coming in from his friends in Norway. "You can do this, big man!" read one. *I hope you're right,* thought Erling, as he saw the crowds gathering outside.

The French team was filled with big-money signings, with Neymar and Kylian Mbappé up front. It meant the Yellow Wall was even louder than normal. The whole ground was a storm of noise. Tonight's match was the first of two legs, and as the Champions League anthem rang around the stands, Erling found his thoughts drifting back to his childhood. In his mind's eye, he saw himself as a tiny boy playing in a City kit in the garden. He smiled and stood tall. That was then. This was now.

The match was tense. Jadon went close after twenty-six minutes, then Erling snatched at a half-chance a few minutes later. The fans oohed and aahed. PSG looked dangerous on the break, but at half-time it was still nil-nil. Then, on sixty-eight minutes, came the breakthrough. A beautiful lay-off from Erling helped Jadon set Dortmund free on the right. The ball came low into the area, where Dortmund's Raphaël Guerreiro struck a shot goalwards. It hit a defender, bounced up, and there was Erling to poke it home. GOOOOAALLLL!

As the volume inside the ground went into lift-off, Erling celebrated by sliding to the floor and sitting in a meditation pose, before being swamped by his teammates. But their excitement was short-lived – within six minutes, PSG were level through Neymar.

"Keep your heads up!" shouted Manuel Akanji, one of the Dortmund subs, from the bench. "There's still time to win this!"

Two minutes later, as 80,000 fans cheered the team on, Dortmund broke forward. Substitute Gio Reyna received the ball at the halfway line, turned and ran. As space opened up, he slid the ball to Erling, thirty yards out. His first touch was perfect, steadying himself as three defenders closed in. He had a split second to choose his next move. But he knew what to do. Drawing back his left foot, he sent a long-distance screamer rocketing into the top corner. GOOOOAALLLL! 2-1!! A wonder strike in the Champions League!!

The Yellow Wall exploded. Erling ran to the corner flag and collapsed on the ground. As the stadium roared into the night and the TV commentators went wild, he lay flat on his back. Just two years ago, he'd been playing on windy pitches in the Norwegian countryside. Now he was here, the hero on the biggest stage of all, surrounded by deafening crowds. *Please*, he thought, *don't let this stop.*

BORUSSIA DORTMUND

Nickname: The Black & Yellows, The BVB
Founded: December 1909
Current league: German Bundesliga
Current manager: Edin Terzicr
Crest: A yellow circle with black trim, with the letters BVB and the numbers 09 (BVB is short for Ballspiel-Verein Borussia Dortmund, the club's full name; 09 is the date the club was founded)

EMPTY GROUNDS

"It gives you goosebumps," Erling had said in an interview before the PSG match. "To watch the Yellow Wall and to see all these people – it's amazing. And when they chant my name? It's one of the best feelings of my whole life, to be honest."

But it was one of the last times he would play in front of a Dortmund home crowd.

By the time the return leg took place in Paris a month later, the world was dealing with the outbreak of Covid-19. To keep the public safe, fans were banned from going to matches. For a while, it even looked as though football itself would have to be stopped. But the season continued, with games played out in empty stadiums.

"This feels weird," said Jadon, as they warmed up before the match in a silent Parc des Princes.

"You're right," said Erling, firing a shot at the goal. "We just have to keep focused. The fans will still be watching on TV."

But when PSG won 2-0, it meant Dortmund were out of the Champions League, losing 3-2 on aggregate. The team were deflated. It felt as though their season was over. They still had nine league games left, but they had little hope of catching Bayern Munich in the table. And despite going on to win six of their remaining matches, they finished second by thirteen points.

Erling finished the season with sixteen goals from eighteen appearances, but it was hard not to feel disappointed. *Next season we'll win some silverware, he told himself.*

Because of the pandemic, the summer break was a strange one. Erling used the time to recharge. He kept up his meditation, grew his hair and stayed fit. From time to time he rewarded himself with a takeaway kebab pizza – his guilty pleasure – but mostly he relaxed, trained and turned his thoughts to the new season.

"There's a positive feeling in the squad," he said to Astor on the phone one evening. Since Covid-19, he was calling all his family for regular chats, enjoying the familiarity of their voices. "This might be our year."

But the season began with mixed results. Dortmund won seven of their thirteen matches before Christmas, with small crowds now allowed into the grounds. Erling couldn't stop grinning when he saw yellow shirts back in the stands. It wasn't the same as a full stadium, but it was something. Frustratingly though, every time Dortmund looked like getting a run of wins together, things went wrong. Erling and Jadon were still scoring goals – and they loved linking up with new midfielder, Jude Bellingham – but the team were inconsistent. Their heads dropped. The manager was sacked. Assistant coach Edin Terzic stepped in.

This gave them the lift they needed, particularly in the cup competitions. Erling himself was having a blazing season, terrifying defences all over Germany. He had a new nickname now, after a half-man, half-robot from a famous film: the Terminator.

His goals had also put them top of their Champions League group, and he scored another four against Seville to help Dortmund reach the quarter-finals. This was a huge achievement – but it became even better when he saw the draw for the next round.

"No way!" shouted Erling when Jadon texted through the news. "We've been drawn against City!" Rumours had been swirling for months that City and their manager Pep Guardiola had their eyes on Erling as a future signing. That was something he could hardly bring himself to think about, let alone talk about. *Probably just newspaper talk*, he thought. *And right now, I'd do anything for the Black and Yellows.*

But still, when he walked out on to the pitch at City's stadium, his spirit soared. This was a different, newer ground to the one his dad had played in – the club had left Maine Road years ago – but it was City's home. Huge sky-blue stands surrounded him on all sides. It looked awesome.

The match, however, didn't go to plan for Dortmund. The pandemic had reared up again, meaning no fans could attend the game, and the lack of atmosphere seemed to stifle the German team. They lost 2-1, a scoreline that was repeated in the second leg at an empty Westfalenstadion.

Two things were now keeping the season alive for Erling. One, he was still scoring at an amazing rate. It seemed there wasn't a goalkeeper in the land who could keep him out. And two, Dortmund had qualified for the final of the DFB-Pokal Cup, Germany's top cup competition. They would be playing RB Leipzig. Here, at last, was the chance of a big trophy.

The match took place on a clear May evening in Berlin's Olympiastadion. "It's such a shame there are no fans," said Jude, as the players warmed up under lights. Erling and Jadon nodded, but all of them had received thousands of messages of encouragement on social media. They knew how much this meant to the Dortmund supporters.

The team played their hearts out – and the match was a dream. Five minutes in, Jadon fired home a stunner from the edge of the box. Just before the half-hour mark, Erling brushed off the Leipzig defence to make it two. When he added another long-range goal in the eighty-seventh minute to make it 4-1, victory was certain.

"YEEEESSSSS!!!" shouted Erling, as the trophy was hoisted into the air. The Dortmund squad yelled and danced as they celebrated, spraying champagne and singing songs. Personal achievements were great, Erling thought, but team achievements were even sweeter.

FROM DORTMUND TO ENGLAND

After Erling's performances in the 2020-21 season, and despite Dortmund only finishing third, German fans had voted him as the Bundesliga Player of the Season.

"That says everything," said his dad proudly when Erling went home to Bryne over the summer. "Being recognized like that by the fans is a real honour."

By now, the rumours about Manchester City's interest were everywhere. And it wasn't just City. PSG, Real Madrid, Bayern Munich and even Manchester United were all being linked with

Erling too. "I've said it before," said Alfie, grinning as he fired up the barbecue in the garden. "Just keep your feet on the ground and work hard."

Dortmund had appointed a new manager for the following season, Marco Rose, and Erling was optimistic about the year ahead. But, again, things didn't go perfectly.

He started with a bang, scoring a hat-trick in a cup game and two more in the opening league match. Then he was struck by two injuries – first to his hamstring, then his hip – putting him out of action for months. It was so frustrating. With all the noise around his possible transfer, it was sometimes hard for him to focus on what was happening here and now – and even harder when he wasn't playing.

When he returned to the side in November, however, he continued to give a hundred per cent, leaving every ounce of his energy on the pitch. Crowds of 15,000 were now allowed in the stadium, which was a huge boost. He kept up his incredible scoring record until he was hit by yet another injury, this time to his groin. "I can't believe it," he said to the team doctor, tearing off his hairband in frustration. "Three injuries in one season!""

It was March before he was fit again, and just two months of the campaign remained. By now, however, his move to the Premier League was all but confirmed. The Dortmund fans still treated him like a hero, and he was closer than ever to his teammates, but they all knew he wouldn't be pulling on the yellow shirt for much longer.

When he played his final game at Westfalenstadion, against Hertha BSC, the rules around Covid-19 had been loosened. It meant the stadium was packed with 80,000 fans. Erling savoured the roar of the crowd one last time as he walked out with the team. And when Dortmund won a penalty in the second half, he knew what to do. In front of the Yellow Wall, he stepped up and fired it home. Business as usual.

But it was also goodbye. His Dortmund career had finished with sixty-two goals in sixty-seven games in the Bundesliga (eighty-six goals from eighty-nine games in all competitions), the statistics of a superstar. He felt emotional as he waved to the fans, but he had reason to feel excited too. He was on his way to Manchester City, the club he'd supported all his life.

This would be interesting. He'd been a toddler when he was last living in England. Now he was the Terminator.

CITY BOY

As Erling looked down the list of his new teammates, he couldn't stop smiling. The big names came thick and fast. Kevin de Bruyne. Ederson. Bernardo Silva. Jack Grealish. Rodri. The squad was full of born winners. And what about the manager! Pep Guardiola was the best in the world. Erling had been confirmed as a City player just before his twenty-second birthday, and he'd felt as though he was living in a movie ever since.

In an interview just after his arrival, he was asked what he wanted to achieve in Manchester. Typically, he went into joke mode. "First of all, I want to match my dad's career scoring record of eighteen Premier League goals," he said, his eyes twinkling. "He scored three for City. That's my first target."

Wherever he went, City fans were thrilled to see him. On the street he kept spotting "HAALAND 9" replica shirts, and when the club held a special welcome event outside the stadium, thousands turned up to see him. He was brought out on stage to loud cheers. "I want to have fun," he told the crowd. "When I have fun, I score goals. When I score goals, I win games." The cheers grew even louder.

Erling and the fans all knew one of the big reasons why he was here at City. Goals? Sure. Winning games? Naturally. But in all their long history, the club had never won the Champions League. It was the trophy that had always eluded them. Erling, everyone hoped, would be the missing piece in the jigsaw.

As the season approached, Erling seemed relaxed and happy. People were surprised that the pressure of being the most talked-about player in the Premier League didn't seem to be weighing him down. But he was surrounded by his closest friends and family, playing for his favourite club in the world. He was fit, strong and raring to go. What was there to worry about?

When his first game – in the Community Shield at a sold-out Wembley Stadium, against Liverpool – ended in a disappointing loss, he wasn't too concerned. The season was long. In the meantime, he focused on looking after himself: exercising well, eating well and sleeping well. But when he had football boots on his feet, he worked like a monster.

MANCHESTER CITY

Nickname: City, The Citizens, The Sky Blues
Founded: April 1894
Current league: Premier League
Current manager: Pep Guardiola
Crest: A rounded badge with a shield containing a ship and the Lancashire rose, with the words Manchester City and the date 1894.

"Go, go, go!" shouted Pep across the training pitch. It was three days before the first league game, and the manager and coaches were determined to get the squad as fit as possible, pushing them to their limit with exercise drills. Erling gave it everything, sprinting hard, shooting hard and tackling hard. He soon realized that attitude was normal here.

After the drill, he took a swig of water. Kevin and Kyle Walker were practicing their crosses, Bernardo and Phil Foden were tapping quick passes to each other, and Riyad Mahrez and Ilkay Gündoğan were firing bullet shots at Ederson. His old Dortmund teammate Manuel was practicing with them too, having transferred to City at the same time, which was great news.

Jack appeared at Erling's side. The two of them had already realized they lived in the same luxury apartment building. "This is going to be a fun season," said Jack to his new friend. Erling gazed around and saw world-class players in world-class facilities. He bumped fists with Jack. "It really is," he laughed.

True to form, he didn't take long to get his goals

tally started. His Premier League debut was away at West Ham on a sunny day in London. Shortly before half-time, Ilkay played a neat through-ball to Erling, who was brought down by the keeper. Penalty! With the City fans urging him on, he stepped up, slotted the ball into the corner and celebrated with his meditation pose. His wide smile said it all – he was off the mark.

In the sixty-fifth minute, City pushed again. Kevin split the defence with a glorious pass and there was Erling, speeding on to the ball. He opened up his body and passed it coolly into the net. Simple. It was like shooting practice with Coach Berntsen, all those years ago. "Superb, Erling!" said Pep in the changing room. "If you keep this up, who knows what we can achieve!"

Erling took his words to heart. By the end of August, he'd scored nine times in just five Premier League matches, including two home hat-tricks. He was loving being part of such a well-oiled squad. Players like Phil, Ilkay, Jack and Riyad were a dream to play with, but there was one teammate who really shone out.

"Kevin's a genius," he said to his dad, after the

Belgian midfielder had set up Erling's tenth City goal. "The way he threads the ball – wow. We're linking up brilliantly."

Alfie was now spending lots of time in England to be close to his son. This was a real help to Erling, who was already a media sensation. But staying cool and collected was vital, especially as City's first big test of the season was coming up – a home Champions League match against Dortmund.

"This will be intense," said Manuel to Erling in the warm-up. They both knew how good their old team were. For Erling, lining up against Dortmund was a crazy experience. These were his friends – people he'd shared amazing memories with. Now he was trying to beat them, and as soon as the whistle went, winning was his only thought. He chased and harried the Dortmund players, desperate for a chance to score.

His opportunity came late, in the eighty-third minute, with the score at 1-1 and the crowd getting restless. City's João Cancelo had the ball in midfield and looked up. He spotted Erling in the box and delivered a high, hopeful cross.

What happened next was one of those moments

that would live with Erling for ever. With defenders on either side, he gave a giant leap and stretched out his left foot. It was as though he was floating. Somehow he made contact, acrobatically volleying the winner into the roof of the net. A miracle goal!! The crowd erupted but he celebrated without fuss – this was Dortmund, after all. At the final whistle, he rested his arms around his former teammates as he left the pitch. What a night.

The big matches kept on coming. His first Manchester derby was the biggest Premier League match of the season so far. But for this City team? No problem. He and Phil both bagged hat-tricks as they battered United 6-3. The fans sang his name for hours.

Erling's electric talent was now the talk of England. At a packed press conference, he was asked to give the secret to his success. "Ah, that's easy," he said with a laugh. "I have it before every home game. My dad's lasagna."

FOOD & DRINK

Erling loves Alfie's lasagna – but it's not the only food he's crazy about. His favourite takeaway treat is kebab pizza and he's a huge meat-eater. When City won the treble and went to celebrate in a restaurant, he surprised the chefs by walking into the kitchen wearing sky-blue silk pyjamas and asking to cook his own steak! He consumes around 6,000 calories of food a day – most people eat around 2,000! He also thinks a lot about what he drinks. He likes to drink filtered water rather than tap water. He's also spoken about drinking his special "magic potion", which is a milk smoothie mixed with spinach and kale!

TROPHIES UP FOR GRABS

As Erling's debut season in England continued, his name dominated the headlines. Whenever he went a few games without scoring, the newspapers wondered if his form was dropping. Erling knew better. He hated having dry patches, but he always stayed calm and did things his own way. When he wasn't spending time with his friends or teammates, he liked taking ice baths and having massages. He turned up to training one morning with his long hair in pigtails. He even loved wearing silk pyjamas on his days off. When he was asked why, he replied with a smile. "They're comfortable," he said. "I like them."

But he did most of his talking on the pitch – and so did City. By the spring, they were on course for something unforgettable. Erling had broken all kinds of records, scoring more than forty goals. His partnership with Kevin was now feared across Europe. But more importantly, the team were still competing for all three of the biggest trophies: the FA Cup, the Premier League and the top prize of the lot, the Champions League.

The matches that followed contained highlight after highlight. In mid-April, he scored in both Champions League games against Bayern Munich, sending City through to a last-four tie against Real Madrid. Soon afterwards, he helped City knock out Sheffield United in the FA Cup semi-final, thanks to three goals from Riyad. And four days later he scored a ninety-fifth-minute goal to ensure City beat Arsenal, their main rivals for the league title. Erling now had the record for the most Premier League goals in a season! The players, and the fans, were sensing something special. The treble was on.

In training, the squad kept the intensity high. Pep was on the move constantly, shouting instructions. Older players like Kyle, Kevin and Ilkay made sure everyone stayed focused. "This is our time," said Kevin to Erling and Jack, as they all got changed after a mammoth practice session. "The next few weeks are crucial."

First up was the Premier League. While City kept winning, Arsenal stumbled. With three games to spare, Erling and the team had won their first silverware of the season. The famous trophy shone in Ilkay's hands as he lifted it high above his head. Erling put his arms around Kyle and Rodri and looked to the sky. He couldn't believe it – his first season in England and he was a Premier League champion!

"OK," said a beaming Jack, as they walked around the pitch applauding the fans. "One down, two to go."

The Champions League semi-final was up next. After drawing 1-1 in Spain, City demolished Real Madrid 4-0 at home in one of the greatest performances in the club's history. The crowd and the players went delirious as two goals from Bernardo, and a goal apiece from Manuel and Julián Álvarez, sent City into the final against Inter

Milan. It was happening.

Two games to go. Two more trophies to win. The FA Cup Final was an unforgettable day, with City up against their fiercest rivals, Manchester United. Wembley was a sea of blue and red. A headed pass from Erling helped Ilkay give City the lead after just twelve seconds – and after that, there was only going to be one winner. By teatime, as the blue half of the stadium cheered and danced, City had their second trophy of the season.

"We've done the double!" shouted Kyle, as the players returned to the changing room to continue the party. "One more, boys! One more!"

The Champions League final was taking place a week later, way over on the other side of Europe, in the Turkish city of Istanbul. The days leading up to the match dragged slowly. The players tried to keep relaxed at their training sessions, but there was a nerviness in the squad too. "We've got a chance to make history," said Phil to Erling as they practiced quick one-twos. "City have never won this. And imagine doing the treble! I know we can do it." Erling nodded and tried to stay calm. He looked around at his teammates, all training hard, all concentrating. Phil was right.

Finally, matchday arrived. It was a warm Turkish night, with a feeling of magic in the air. As he watched the fans pouring into the stadium, Erling had to pinch himself. This was it. The big one. The trophy he'd fantasized about since he was a boy. The matches he'd watched on TV with his dad. The music he'd woken up to for years. And he was here as City's number nine.

As the stands echoed with chants and Pep gave them one last team-talk in the changing room, Erling looked around at the faces he'd got to know over the season. Faces he trusted. Some of these players had lost the Champions League final just two years earlier. Their determined expressions told Erling that this wouldn't happen again.

When the whistle sounded, he felt a strange mix of emotions. His thoughts flashed back to Bryne, to Molde, to Salzburg, to Dortmund. It all led here.

The match, though, was tight and nervy. Erling had a difficult chance in the first half, but by half-time neither side was on top.

In the sixty-eighth minute, it happened. Manuel and Bernardo combined to set up a chance for Rodri, who blasted it home. 1-0!! The players piled on top of each other. The fans were ecstatic. The final part of the game saw City clinging on desperately, with Ederson producing some superhuman saves. When the final whistle came, Erling was stunned. As the pitch filled with coaches and players, all screaming and shouting, he was in a daze. The tears came streaming down. They'd done it, for the first time in City's history. The Champions League. The treble. And in his first season!

The rest was a blur. He hugged Pep. He hugged Kevin, Jack and Manuel. He hugged his family. He hugged anyone he saw, and his smile never faded. His dad was happier than he'd ever seen him before. As the world looked on and the City fans sang late into the night, Erling watched the celebrations unfold around him. He took a deep breath. He'd scored fifty-two goals this season and earned three winners' medals – including the Champions League.

He was going to enjoy the next few weeks to the full, but it didn't feel like an ending. It felt like a beginning.

The future's bright, he thought, as his teammates

dragged him into a mass of dancing blue shirts, *and there's much more to come from the boy from Bryne.*

Haaland Timeline

21 July 2000	Erling Braut Haaland is born in Leeds, England.
2004	He leaves England with his family to move to their hometown of Bryne, in Norway.
2006	He breaks the world record for his age for the standing long jump.
2006/7	He begins attending training sessions at the Bryne FK academy, his dad's old team.
2015	He is selected for the Norway Under-15 squad, scoring an incredible goal from the halfway line against Sweden.

2015	He is promoted to play in the Bryne FK reserve team, netting eighteen goals in fourteen games.
12 May 2016	He makes his first-team debut for Bryne FK against Ranheim, two months before his sixteenth birthday.
1 February 2017	He is signed by Norwegian top-flight club Molde, managed by the legendary former striker Ole Gunnar Solskjaer.
1 July 2018	He scores four goals in the opening twenty-one minutes against Brann, one of the performances that earns him the Breakthrough Player of the Year award in Norway's top league.
1 January 2019	He joins the Austrian champions RB Salzburg. Despite being at the club for less than a year, he scores five hat-tricks and finds the net in five consecutive Champions League matches.

30 May 2019	He scores nine goals for Norway in their 12-0 victory against Honduras at the FIFA Under-20 World Cup in Poland, winning the tournament's Golden Boot.
28 August 2019	He is named in the senior Norway squad for the first time, making his debut against Malta on 5 September.
29 December 2019	He transfers to the German Bundesliga club Borussia Dortmund, where he spends two and a half seasons.
18 January 2020	He makes his Dortmund debut as a substitute against Augsburg, scoring a hat-trick in twenty-three minutes to turn the match around.
18 February 2020	He scores both goals as Dortmund beat PSG in the first leg of a Champions League last-sixteen match.

4 September 2020	He scores his first goal for the senior Norway team in a match against Austria.
6 March 2021	At the age of twenty, he scores the hundredth goal of his senior club career, in a match against Bayern Munich.
13 May 2021	He scores twice to help Dortmund win the DFB-Pokal Final in Berlin. At the end of the season, he is named Bundesliga Player of the Year.
27 November 2021	He becomes the youngest ever Bundesliga player to score fifty goals.
10 May 2022	He joins Manchester City, the club he has supported all his life, for a fee of around fifty-one million pounds.
7 August 2022	He scores twice on his league debut, against West Ham United.

28 December 2022	He scores twice against Leeds United, becoming the fastest ever player to reach twenty Premier League goals.
14 March 2023	He scores five times in one Champions League match, against RB Leipzig.
18 March 2023	In a FA Cup match against Burnley, he scores his sixth hat-trick of the season.
14 May 2023	He scores his fifty-second and final goal of the season across all competitions, in a league match against Everton. It is by far the most goals ever scored for City in a single season.
20 May 2023	He celebrates as City are confirmed as Premier League Champions, due to rivals Arsenal losing 1-0 against Nottingham Forest.

3 June 2023	He helps City beat Manchester United 2-1 in the FA Cup Final, securing the club's second ever league and cup double.
10 June 2023	He helps City beat Inter Milan 1-0 in the UEFA Champions League Final in Istanbul, confirming the treble.

Team Trophies

2018/19	Austrian Bundesliga, Austrian Cup (RB Salzburg – joined midway through season)
2019/20	Austrian Bundesliga, Austrian Cup (RB Salzburg – left midway through season)
2020/21	DFB-Pokal Cup (Borussia Dortmund)
2022/23	Premier League, FA Cup, UEFA Champions League (Manchester City)

Personal Awards

2019	FIFA Under-20 World Cup Golden Boot
2019	Austrian Bundesliga Player of the Year
2020	Golden Boy Award for best young footballer in Europe
2020	Norwegian Footballer of the Year
2020/21	UEFA Champions League top scorer
2020/21	UEFA Nations League top scorer
2020/21	German Bundesliga Player of the Season

2021	Norwegian Footballer of the Year
2022	Norwegian Footballer of the Year
2022/23	Premier League Golden Boot
2022/23	UEFA Champions League top scorer
2022/23	UEFA Champions League Goal of the Season (for volley against Dortmund)
2022/23	Premier League Player of the Season
2022/23	Premier League Young Player of the Season
2022/23	Football Writers' Association Player of the Season
2022/23	European Golden Shoe

What they say about Erling

"I think he has changed everything. He was born for this, scoring goals, and he is going to break all of the records for sure." – City player Rodri

"We have got the best striker in the world playing up front who is just obsessed with scoring goals. He is honestly a brilliant person to be around. I cannot speak highly enough of him. He's a great guy." – City player Jack Grealish

"He's absolutely phenomenal. I can't keep up with counting; he just seems to score goal after goal. He loves big games." – Former City striker Shaun Goater

"He's incredible, also as a person as well. We know how good he is. He's so prolific in front of the net and it's deserved. He's clinical when he gets these chances and I'm really happy for him. He is also unselfish at times because not even Erling is going to score in every game – that's impossible – he knows the team always comes first." – City player John Stones

"He's a beast! And it looks to me as though he has got his dad's impish smile. He looks as though he is enjoying himself, so long may it last." – Former City manager Joe Royle

"The big man brings goals." – City player Kyle Walker

What Erling says

"It's a really good thing, to relax, to try to not think too much. Because stress is not good for anyone. I hate to be stressed, and I try not to be stressed."

"As soon as I score a goal, all I can think about is getting the next one. That is how I approach this situation and will continue to."

"It's always about believing in yourself, trying to enjoy every single day – both as a football player and as a person. I try to smile as much as I can."

"Being a well-known footballer means you have to

adapt a little bit in your lifestyle and how you do things, but I try to live as normally as I can. I try to do the same things that I did as a teenager in my hometown. I try to live as normally as possible."

"Be kind, be generous, be comprehensive – but most of all, be thankful."

Record Breaker

Erling's debut season with City in 2022/2023 saw him smash all sorts of records:

Most goals ever scored for City in one season: **52**

Most Champions League goals ever scored for City in one season: **10**

First player in history to score in his first four away Premier League games

First player in history to score hat-tricks in three consecutive home Premier League games

Fastest player in history to reach 10 Premier League goals: 6 games

Fastest player in history to reach 25 Premier League goals: **19 games**

Fastest player in history to reach 30 Champions League goals: **25 games**

Most goals in history in a Premier League season: **36**

The phenomenal 52-goal season

35 goals with his left foot
9 with his right foot
8 with his head
20 in the six-yard box
31 in the penalty area
1 outside the penalty area
9 assists
6 hat-tricks

Erling's assistants

Who provided the assists for Erling's 52 goals in the 2022/23 season?

12: Kevin de Bruyne

4: Phil Foden, Jack Grealish

3: Riyad Mahrez, João Cancelo, John Stones

2: Ilkay Gündoğan

1: Sergio Gomez, Rodri, Bernardo Silva, Julián Álvarez, Ederson (yes, the goalkeeper!)

16: No assist

Playing for Norway

From the day he was called up for the Norway Under-15 team, Erling has been a consistent member of his country's international squads. He played for the Under-15s, the Under-16s, the Under-17s, the Under-18s, the Under-19s, the Under-20s and the Under-21s!

But his proudest moments have come while playing for the full senior team. By the end of the 2022/23 season, he had played twenty-five times, scoring twenty-four goals. On 11 October 2020, he got his first international hat-trick when he scored three times against Romania.

Fascinatingly, because he was born in Leeds, he could have chosen to play for England! Instead, he opted to pull on the red shirt of Norway, just like his dad before him.

Erling's Clubs

Bryne FK

Club name: Bryne FK

Nickname: Jaerens Superlag (the Super Team from the Jaerens Region)

Founded: April 1926

Current league: Norwegian First Division

Current manager: Kevin Knappen

Crest: A red globe in a white shield on the outline of a green leaf, with the words 'Bryne FK'

Molde FK

Club name: Molde FK

Nickname: MFK

Founded: June 1911

Current league: Eliteserien (Norwegian Premier League)

Current manager: Erling Moe

Crest: A blue oval with white trim, with the letters MFK and the numbers 19/6/1911 (the date the club was founded)

RB Salzburg

Club name: RB Salzburg

Nickname: Die Roten Bullen (The Red Bulls)

Founded: September 1933

Current league: Austrian Bundesliga

Current manager: Gerhard Struber

Crest: A white shield with black trim under a yellow star, with two bulls charging towards a football

Borussia Dortmund

Club name: Borussia Dortmund

Nickname: The Black & Yellows, The BVB

Founded: December 1909

Current league: German Bundesliga

Current manager: Edin Terzicr

Crest: A yellow circle with black trim, with the letters BVB and the numbers 09 (BVB is short for Ballspiel-Verein Borussia Dortmund, the club's full name; 09 is the date the club was founded)

Manchester City

Club name: Manchester City

Nickname: City, The Citizens, The Sky Blues

Founded: April 1894

Current league: Premier League

Current manager: Pep Guardiola

Crest: A rounded badge with a shield containing a ship and the Lancashire rose, with the words Manchester City and the date 1894.

Family Talent

His dad Alfie isn't the only other family member to shine on the football pitch. Erling's younger cousins Jonatan Braut Brunes and Albert Tjaland are both professional footballers too.

Jonatan, who started out at Bryne like Erling, is a striker who played for the Norwegian top-flight team Stromsgodset. He moved to the Belgian team OH Leuven on 14 August 2023.

Albert is also a striker and currently plays for Molde, another of Erling's old clubs.

Fun Erling Facts!

He's amazingly quick for such a tall player. He sprinted so fast in his Champions League game against PSG in 2020 that he reached a speed of 36 km/h!

Erling has a lot in common with another speedy superstar, the French striker Kylian Mbappe. They're both incredibly skilful big-match players scoring countless goals. People often say they're going to be the new Ronaldo and Messi!

When Erling scored five goals for City against RB Leipzig in the Champions League, it took him just fifty-seven minutes. He bagged two with his left, two with his right and one with his head! The only other players to score five goals in one Champions League game are Luiz Adriano and Lionel Messi, who both needed more than eighty minutes.

Erling keeps all the match balls from the games where he's scored a hat-trick. He once even claimed that he went to sleep with them in his bed! When Erling and Phil Foden both scored hat-tricks in the same match against Manchester United, they kept a match ball each.

When Erling spent the first few years of his life in England, he developed a taste for British sweets. Even today, his favourite sweets are still Percy Pigs!

The rap video that Erling and his friends made when he was a youngster in Bryne can still be watched on the internet. It's called "Kygo Jo" by the Flow Kingz, and features a young Erling rapping in front of a barbecue grill!

One of the ways that Erling relaxes is by playing video games. He once refused to say what his favourite game was, claiming it was a bit too embarrassing, but soon afterwards he posted a picture of himself on social media playing Minecraft!

The Numbers Game

Erling wears the prestigious number nine shirt for City, following in the footsteps of past players like Gabriel Jesus, Paulo Wanchope, Niall Quinn, Brian Kidd, Francis Lee and Joe Royle.

He also wore the number nine for Dortmund in the 2020/21 and 2021/22 seasons, although when he first joined the club he was given the number seventeen.

At RB Salzburg, he wore the number thirty shirt, which was also the number he wore at Molde. Beginning his career at Bryne, he wore the number nineteen shirt.

Also available in the Football Legends series:

FOOTBALL LEGENDS
TAMMY ABRAHAM
Matt Whyman

FOOTBALL LEGENDS
KYLIAN MBAPPÉ
Ed Hawkins

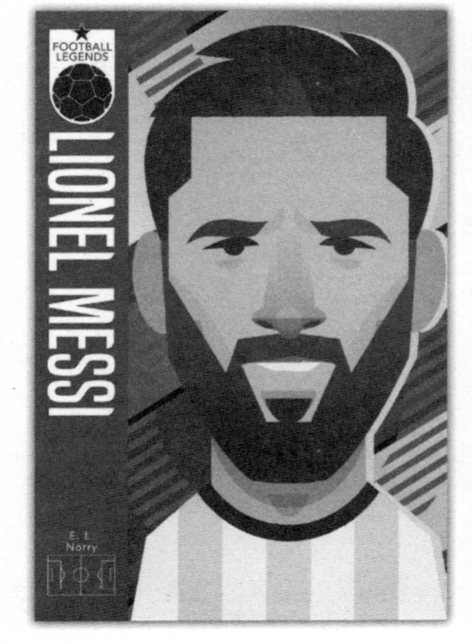
FOOTBALL LEGENDS
LIONEL MESSI
E. L. Norry

FOOTBALL LEGENDS
GARETH SOUTHGATE
E. L. Norry